CW00728447

Jill ve Fasulye Sarmaşığı

Jill and the Beanstalk

by Manju Gregory
illustrated by David Anstey

Turkish translation by Talin Altun

mantra

Jack kardeşi Jill ile bir bayırı tırmandı,
Jack şimdi hasta çünkü aşağı yuvarlandı.
Yiyecek yok, herkes mutsuz,
Keşke Dev babalarını yutmamış olsaydı.

Jack climbed a hill with his sister Jill.
Jack fell down and now he's ill.
There's nothing to eat, they're feeling sad,
If only the Giant hadn't swallowed their dad.

Annesi Jill'e sordu,
"Acaba ineğimizi satsan paramız olur mu?"

Mum asked Jill, "Do you think somehow
You could raise money selling our cow?"

Jill henüz çok yürümemişti ki çitin kenarında bir adam gördü.
"İneğini bu fasulyelere değişirim," dedi.
"Fasulye mi?" dedi Jill. "Sen dalga geçiyorsun benimle!"
Adam anlattı, "Bunlar sihirli fasulye. Hiç görmediğin hediyeler getirirler."

Jill had barely walked a mile when she met a man beside a stile.
"Swap you these beans for that cow," he said.
"Beans!" cried Jill. "Are you off your head?"
The man explained, "These are magic beans. They bring you gifts you've never seen."

Jill eve gitti, annesine göstermek için fasulyeleri.
O da "Oğlumu göndermem gerekirdi!" dedi.
Fasulyeleri yere fırlatıp
Jilli aç susuz yatağa yolladı.

Jill took them home to show her mum
Who cried out loud, "I should have sent my son!"
She threw the beans down at Jill's feet
And sent her to bed with nothing to eat.

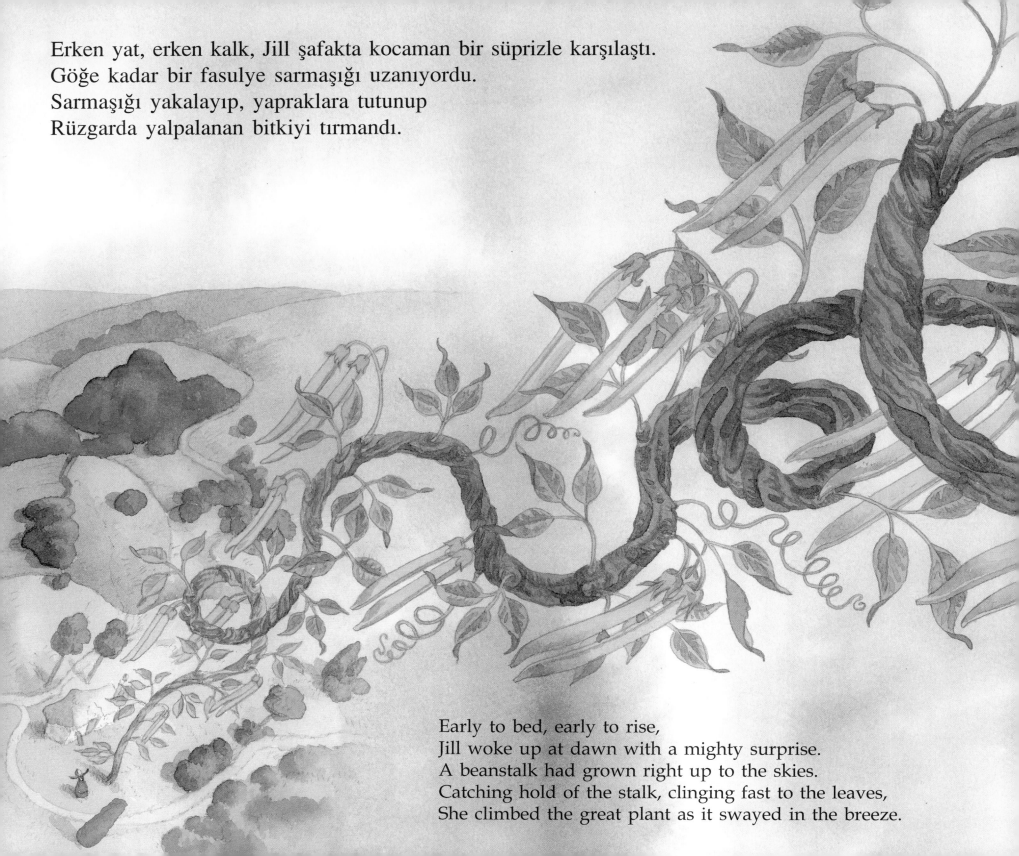

Erken yat, erken kalk, Jill şafakta kocaman bir süprizle karşılaştı.
Göğe kadar bir fasulye sarmaşığı uzanıyordu.
Sarmaşığı yakalayıp, yapraklara tutunup
Rüzgarda yalpalanan bitkiyi tırmandı.

Early to bed, early to rise,
Jill woke up at dawn with a mighty surprise.
A beanstalk had grown right up to the skies.
Catching hold of the stalk, clinging fast to the leaves,
She climbed the great plant as it swayed in the breeze.

Jill bir ses duydu, Annesi olmalıydı.
"Hemen aşağı in, kardeşine göz kulak ol!"
Ama Jill tırmanmaya devam etti
Hiç durmadan tepeye kadar gitti.

Jill heard a shout, it was her mother!
"Come down at once, look after your brother!"
But Jill just kept on climbing, she didn't stop,
All the way upwards, right to the top.

Jill sarmaşıktan atladı, bir ağlama sesi duydu.
Küçük bir kız "Koyunlarım nerede?" diyordu.
"Ben uyurken kaçmış olmalılar."
"Ben nerdeyim?" diye sordu Jill.

She leapt off the beanstalk, and heard a loud weep.
A little girl cried, "Oh, where are my sheep?
They've wandered away while I was asleep."
"Where am I?" asked Jill.

"Devin yaşadığı diyardasın."
Öç almaya mı affetmeye mi geldin?
Değneğimi salla ve kaderini seç.
Ya sarmaşıktan aşağı ya da Devin kapısından içeri.

"You're in the land where the Giant lives.
Did you come to avenge or come to forgive?
With a wave of my crook now choose your fate,
Back down the beanstalk or onto the Giant's Gate?"

Küçük bir fare gibi korkup titreyerek
Jill Devin evinin önünde durdu.
Garip, yaşlı bir kadın duruyordu yakında,
Gökteki örümcek ağlarını temizliyordu.
"Küçük kız, neden buradasın? Neden, neden?"

Jill stood in front of the Giant's house
Feeling tiny and scared like a quivering mouse.
A strange old woman was standing by,
Brushing cobwebs out of the sky.
"Little girl, why are you here? Why, oh why?"

Konuşmaya başlayınca muazzam bir deprem oluyormuş gibi yer gürledi.
Kadın "Çabuk, içeriye koş. Saklanacak tek bir yer var…fırının içine gir,
Sakın nefes alma, ses çıkarma. Ölmek istemiyorsan kar kadar sessiz ol," dedi.

As she spoke the ground began to shake, with a deafening sound like a mighty earthquake.
The woman said, "Quick run inside. There's only one place…in the oven you'll hide!
Take barely one breath, don't utter a sigh, stay silent as snow, if you don't want to die."

Jill fırına girdi. Ne yapıyordu? Keşke evde annesiyle olsaydı.

Dev konuştu, "Fi, fay, fo, fam. Dünyalı birinin kanını kokluyorum."

"Kocacığım, sen yemeğinin içindeki kuşların kokusunu alıyorsun. Yirmi dördü de gökten düştü."

Jill crouched in the oven. What had she done? How she wished she were home with her mum.

The Giant spoke, "Fee, fi, faw, fum. I smell the blood of an earthly man."

"Husband, you smell only the birds I baked in a pie. All four and twenty dropped out of the sky."

Dev "Senin yaptığın zarif yemeğe
dokunmam bile. Bir şeyler yemem gerekiyor.
Hemen mutfaktan et getir," diye haykırdı.
Fırının kapısının aralığından, Jill Devin yabandomuzunu nasıl
silip süpürdüğünü seyretti.

The Giant bawled, "I have no wish to even try your dainty dish.
Wife, I need to eat. Go to the kitchen and fetch me my meat!"
From a gap in the oven door, Jill watched the Giant devour a wild boar.

Dev arkasına yaslandı, hiç mutlu değildi.
"Bana kazımı getir, ayağını da çabuk tut."
"Kaz yumurtla" diyerek gözlerini kapadı.
Kaz parlak altın bir yumurta yumurtladı.
Jill çok şaşırdı.
Saf altın yumartaları tek tek sayarken,
Dev de baya bir eğlendi.
Sonra uyuya kalıp horlamaya başladı.
Sanki bir aslan kükrüyordu.

The Giant sat back, he wasn't happy.
He bellowed: "Get me my goose,
and make it snappy."
Saying, "Goose deliver," he closed his eyes.
It lay a bright golden egg,
much to Jill's surprise.
The Giant had a lot of fun,
Counting solid gold eggs one by one.
Then he fell asleep and started to snore
Sounding just like a mighty lion's roar!

Dev uyurken Jill kaçabileceğini biliyordu.
Yavaşça fırından dışarı çıktı.
Sonra arkadaşı Tom'u hatırladı.
O bir domuz alıp kaçmıştı.
Jill kazı yakalayıp çok hızlı koştu.
"Hemen sarmaşığa gitmeliyim."

Jill knew she could escape while the Giant slept.
So carefully out of the oven she crept.
Then she remembered what her friend, Tom, had done.
Stole a pig and away he'd run.
Grabbing the goose, she ran and ran.
"I must get to that beanstalk as fast as I can."

Hemen aşağı kaydı ve "Ben geldim," dedi.
Annesi ve Jack evden dışarı koştu.

She slid down the stalk shouting, "I'm back!"
And out of the house came mother and Jack.

Ağabeyin ve ben çok meraklandık. Nasıl sarmaşığı göğe kadar tırmandın?"
"Ama anne," dedi Jill, "Hiç zarar görmedim. Ve bak yanımda da ne getirdim."
"Kaz yumurtla" diye Devin sözlerini tekrarladı Jill.
Ve kaz anında parlak altın bir yumurta yumurtladı.

"We've been worried sick, your brother and I. How could you climb that great stalk to the sky?"
"But Mum," Jill said, "I came to no harm. And look what I have under my arm."
"Goose deliver," Jill repeated the words that the Giant had said,
And the goose instantly laid a bright golden egg.

Jill'in Deve yaptığı ziyaret ailesini açlık ve sefaletten kurtardı.

Jill's visit to the Giant's lair kept her family from hunger and despair.

Jack kardeşi Jilli kıskanıyordu.
Keşke bir bayır yerine samaşık tırmanmış olsaydı diye düşünüyordu.
Jack çok övünüyordu.
Devle o karşılaşmış olsaydı kafasını keseceğini söylüyordu.

Jack couldn't help feeling envious of his sister Jill.
He wished he'd climbed a beanstalk instead of a hill.
Jack boasted a lot and often said
If he'd met the Giant he would've chopped off his head.

Anneleri sarmaşığı tırmanmamaları hakkında onları uyarmıştı
Ama Jill Jack'in boş laflarından çok sıkılmıştı.
Bir gün, kılık değiştirerek, Jill sarmaşığı tırmandı
Ve göğe vardı.

Their mother had warned them not to climb that stalk
But Jill was fed up with Jack's idle talk.
One day, in clever disguise, Jill climbed up the beanstalk
And reached the skies.

Yaşlı kadın çitin kenarında oturmuştu mutsuzca.
Dev ona çok ama çok kötü davranıyordu.
Kazı çalındığından beri
Her gün daha da acımasız oluyordu.

The old woman sat by the gate looking sad,
The evil Giant treated her bad, very bad.
He'd become more gruesome by the day,
Since his goose had been stolen away.

Devin karısı Jilli tanımadı.
Ama gürültülü adımların yaklaştığını duydu.
"Dev geliyor. Kokunu alırsa seni kesin öldürür."

The Giant's wife didn't recognise Jill,
But she heard the sound of thundering footsteps coming down the hill.
"The Giant!" she cried. "If he smells your blood now, he's sure to kill."

"Tik, tak, tok.
Çabuk saatin içine saklan!"

"Hickory dickory dock,
Quick, go hide in the clock!"

"Fi, fay, fo, fam. Dünyalı birinin kanını kokluyorum.
İster canlı olsun ister ölü, onun kafasını keseceğim," dedi Dev.
"Taze pişmiş turtalarımın kokusunu alıyorsun yalnızca.
Tarifini Kupa Kraliçesinden ödünç aldım."
"Ben bir Devim kadın. Mutfağa koş ve bana et getir."

"Fe fi faw fum, I smell the blood of an earthly man.
Let him be alive or let him be dead, I'll chop off his head," the Giant said.
"You smell only my freshly baked tarts, I borrowed a recipe from the Queen of Hearts."
"I'm a Giant, wife, I need to eat. Go to the kitchen and get me my meat."

Yine Dev et yedi.
Bir saat geçti ve yenisini istedi.
Karısı saf altından yapılmış, yüz tane teli olan
Bir harp getirdi.
Dev "ÇAL" diye emretti. Çok sıkılmıştı.
Harp aniden kendiliğinden çalmaya başladı.

The Giant gorged on beast as before.
One full hour passed by, then he called for more.
His wife brought in a harp, the most magnificent of things,
Made out of pure gold with a hundred strings.
The Giant yelled: "Play," he was feeling bored.
The harp instantly played of its own accord.

Sakin ve tatlı bir ninni çaldı, ve Dev uyuya kaldı.
Jill kendiliğinden çalan harpı çok istiyordu.
Saatten dışarı yavaşça çıktı ve Dev uyurken altın harpı kaptı.

A lullaby so calm and sweet, the lumbering Giant fell fast asleep.
Jill wanted the harp that played without touch. She wanted it so very much!
Out of the clock she nervously crept, and grabbed the harp of gold whilst the Giant slept.

Sarmaşığa varmaktı Jillin amacı. Yolda dönüp duran bir köpeğe takıldı ayağı.
Harp "EFENDİ! EFENDİ" diye bağırınca Dev kalkıp onları kovalamaya başladı.
Jill çok hızlı koşmak zorunda olduğunun farkındaydı.

To the beanstalk Jill was bound, tripping over a dog, running round and round.
When the harp cried out: "MASTER! MASTER!" The Giant awoke, got up and ran after.
Jill knew she would have to run faster and faster.

Dev inledi "Demek koşabileceğini zannediyorsun!
Bak arkadaşın Tom'un başına neler geldi!"
Harpa sıkıca tutunarak Jill koşmaya devam etti.
"Sarmaşığa çok çabuk gitmeliyim."

The Giant howled, "So you think you can run!
Look what happened to Tom, the piper's son!"
Holding onto the harp, Jill ran and ran,
"I must get to that beanstalk as fast as I can."

Sarmaşıktan aşağı kaydı, harp "EFENDİ!" dedi.
Çirkin Dev yakından takip ediyordu.
Jill baltayı eline aldı
Ve sarmaşığı tek bir darbeyle kesti.

She slid down the stalk, the harp cried: "MASTER!"
The great ugly Giant came thundering after.
Jill grabbed the axe for cutting wood
And hacked down the beanstalk as fast as she could.

Devin her adımı sarmaşığı titretiyordu. Jillin tek darbesi Devi düşürüyordu.
Dev aşağı doğru devrildi.
Jack, Jill ve Anneleri şaşkınlıkla izledi, Dev on metre yerin dibine geçti.

Each Giant's step caused the stalk to rumble. Jill's hack of the axe caused the Giant to tumble.
Down down the Giant plunged!
Jack, Jill and mum watched in wonder, as the giant CRASHED, ten feet under.

Jack, Jill ve Anneleri artık günlerini
Harpın çaldığı şarkıları söyleyerek geçiriyordu.

Jack, Jill and their mother now spend their days,
Singing songs and rhymes that the golden harp plays.

Text copyright © 2004 Manju Gregory
Illustrations copyright © 2004 David Anstey
Dual language copyright © 2004 Mantra
All rights reserved

British Library Cataloguing-in-Publication Data:
a catalogue record for this book is available
from the British Library.

First published 2004 by Mantra
5 Alexandra Grove, London N12 8NU, UK
www.mantralingua.com

"Below are the nursery rhymes mentioned in the story. How many do you know?
Can you still recite them, even a tiny bit? Or do you know a rhyme in another language?
Why not send your rhymes by email to Jamie@mantralingua.com.
We will publish the best ones on our website, www.mantralingua.com. Good luck!" Manju

1. Jack and Jill
Jack and Jill went up the hill
To fetch a pail of water
Jack fell down and broke his crown
And Jill came tumbling after.

Then up Jack got and home did trot
As fast as he could caper
Went to bed and plastered his head
With vinegar and brown paper.

Then Jill came in and she did grin
To see Jack's paper plaster
Her mother whipped her across her knee
For laughing at Jack's disaster.

2. There was a crooked man
There was a crooked man, and he walked a crooked mile,
He found a crooked sixpence against the crooked style;
He bought a crooked cat, which caught a crooked mouse
And they all lived together in a little crooked house.

3. Early to Bed
Early to bed, early to rise,
Makes a man healthy, wealthy and wise.

4. Little Bo Peep
Little Bo Peep has lost her sheep
And can't tell where to find them;
Leave them alone, and they'll come home
And bring their tails behind them.

Little Bo Peep fell fast asleep
And dreamt as she heard them bleating;
But when she awoke, she found it a joke
For they were still all fleeting.

Then up she took her little crook
Determined for to find them;
She found them indeed, but it made her heart bleed,
For they left their tails behind them.

4. Little Bo Peep (continued)
It happened one day, as Bo Peep did stray
Into a meadow hard by
There she espied their tail side by side
All hung on a tree to dry.

She heaved a sigh, and wiped her eye
And over the hillocks went rambling
And tried what she could, as a shepherdess should
To tack again each to its lambkin.

5. There was an old woman tossed up in a basket
There was an old woman tossed up in a basket
Seventeen times as high as the moon.
Where she was going I couldn't but ask it
For in her hand she carried a broom.
"Old woman, old woman, old woman," quoth I,
"Where are you going to up so high?"
"To brush the cobwebs off the sky!"
"May I go with you?"
"Aye, by and by."

6. Sing a Song of Sixpence
Sing a song of sixpence
A pocket full of rye
Four and twenty blackbirds
Baked in a pie.

When the pie was opened
The birds began to sing
Was that not a dainty dish
To set before the King?

The King was in his counting house
Counting out his money;
The Queen was in the parlour,
Eating bread and honey.

The maid was in the garden
Hanging out the clothes,
There came a little blackbird
And snapped off her nose.

7. Hickory Dickory Dock
Hickery dickory dock
A mouse ran up the clock
The clock struck one
The mouse ran down
Hickory dickory dock.

8. Tom, Tom, the Piper's Son
Tom, Tom, the Piper's Son
Stole a pig and away he run;
The pig was eat
And Tom was beat
And Tom went howling down the street.

9. The Queen of Hearts
The Queen of Hearts
She made some tarts
All on a summer's day.
The Knave of Hearts
He stole the tarts
And took them clean away.

The King of Hearts
Called for the tarts
And beat the Knave full sore
The Knave of Hearts
Brought back the tarts
And vowed he steal no more.

10. The little black dog ran round a house
The little black dog ran round the house
And set the bull a-roaring.
And drove the monkey in the boat,
Who set the oars a-rowing.
And scared of the cock upon the rock
Who cracked his throat with crowing.